Bob and Flo

PLAY HIDE-AND-SEEK

Rebecca Ashdown

HOUGHTON MIFFLIN HARCOURT

Boston   New York

It was a rainy day.

Bob came to preschool
with his umbrella.

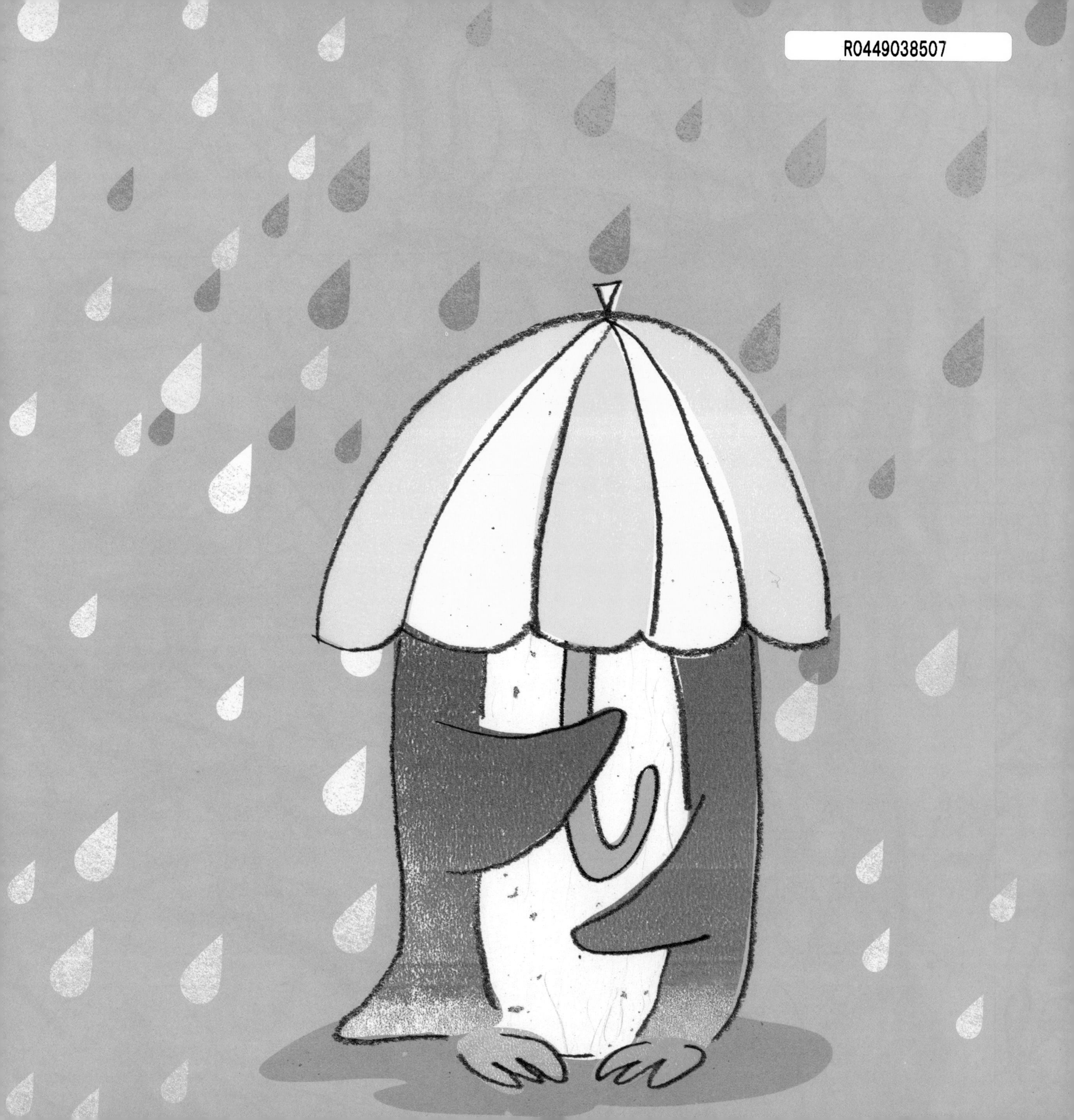

"Hello," said Bob.

"Oh, hello!" said Flo and Sam.

"We didn't see you hiding under there!"

Bob and Flo and Sam decided
to play hide-and-seek.

"I'll hide first,"
said Bob.

Counting to twenty is hard.
So Flo and Sam counted to ten.
Twice!

Bob found a good
place to hide . . .

but Flo and Sam found
him right away.

"You have to hide behind
something," said Sam.

So Bob tried again.

But he was still too easy to find.

"You have to disappear," said Flo.

"One more try!" said Bob.

"Maybe Bob needs more
time to hide," said Sam.

So, as they waited, Flo and Sam played
in the kitchen corner . . .

while Bob thought very hard . . .

about how to disappear.

"Ready or not,
here we come!"
said Flo and Sam.

But where was Bob?

Nowhere!

"Here I am!"

"You disappeared, Bob!"
said Flo and Sam.
"Wonderful hiding!"

And Bob thought Flo and Sam's cake
was wonderful too.

For Alice, Samson, and Anabel

Text and illustrations copyright © 2015 by Rebecca Ashdown
First published in the UK by Oxford University Press in 2015 as *Bob and Flo: Hide and Seek*
First published in the United States in 2016 by Houghton Mifflin Harcourt

www.hmhco.com

The text type was set in Triplex Light.
The display type was set in Fredericka the Great.

Library of Congress Cataloging-in-Publication Data is available.
ISBN 978-0-544-59631-3

Manufactured in China
SCP 10 9 8 7 6 5 4 3 2 1
4500510688